EVENING
An Appalachian Lullaby

For Rachel and Lesley, and in memory of their grandfather, Joseph Alfred Livers, the best lullaby-maker of all

Copyright © 1995 by Paulette Livers Lambert
International Standard Book Number 1-57098-012-8
Library of Congress Catalog Card Number 95-69276

Published by
ROBERTS RINEHART PUBLISHERS
5455 Spine Road, Boulder, Colorado 80301

Published in the UK and Ireland by
ROBERTS RINEHART PUBLISHERS
Trinity House, Charleston Road
Dublin 6, Ireland

Distributed in the U.S. and Canada by Publishers Group West
Printed in Hong Kong

Evening is coming.
The sun sinks to rest.
Mama crow's flying
straight home to her nest.

"Caw!" says the crow
as she flies overhead,
"It's high time that someone
was going to bed!"

Daylily's closing.
Daisy moos deep.
Baby wants to play
a little hide and seek.

Katydids argue:
"Katydid! Katydidn't!"
Cicadas fiddle on,
but they all stay hidden.

Fat possum grins,
her babies all fed.
It's high time that someone
was going to bed.

All the other critters will soon close their eyes, but treefrogs keep croaking their creaky lullabies.

White wheel of moon
rolls up through the sky,
waking up dreams
that are ready to fly.

So wink at the moon
and the stars overhead.
It's high time that someone
was going to bed.

Whippoorwill's crooning
her sweet old song.
Sleepy eyes can't stay
open for long.

Goodnight, little critters!
Big Moon, Goodnight!
Blow us a kiss, now
and put out the light.

Evening has come.
No more to be said.
Goodnight to us all . . .

EVENING
AN APPALACHIAN LULLABY